THE GRIZZLIES' CAPTIVE MATE

ASPEN RIDGE PACK: THE LONERS
BOOK 2

LUNA WILDER

*

They've found her. Now they need to figure out how to keep her.

I thought that meeting Bo and Liam on the street when I was desperate for a job and a place to live was a dream come true.

Turns out, I couldn't have been more wrong about that.

The job that they offered doesn't exist.

Instead, they want me to stay with them. They want be to be their fated mate.

Too bad for them, I just left one controlling man and I'm not about to trade that in for two of them.

Only before I can make my escape, I find myself trapped with them.

Now I'm stuck here, trying to keep a wall between me and the two big men but it's starting to crumble.

With each day that I spend here, I'm left wondering if this is Stockholm Syndrome or something more.

Something like love.

Now that they've found their fated one, they're determined to keep her.

This is an MFM steamy shifter romance! If you love forced proximity, fated mates books where the alpha hero is obsessed with his curvy woman, or in this case, their curvy woman, then you will love The Grizzlies Captive Mate! One click and enjoy today!

ONE

Bo

"DON'T LET me forget to get garlic," I tell Liam, and he nods as we continue to walk toward town.

We're headed to the Aspen Ridge Market to pick up a few things. We do it every Wednesday. It's part of our routine. I think that it keeps Liam sane. He's always liked routine and order, but it's starting to drive me crazy.

I'm starting to hate the monotony of my life.

I wish that we could find our fated mate already.

My bear nods his head inside me. I knew that he would agree. When Liam and I decided to stop looking for our mate a few months ago, he hated the idea. He had growled and paced inside of me for weeks, trying to get me to change my mind, but I hadn't.

Liam and I have been all over the world looking for her in the last five years. We haven't had any luck and it was starting to depress the hell out of both of us. We can both only get our hopes up so many times before it will break us.

When Liam suggested taking a break, I agreed because I could see he needed it. We've always been as close as brothers. We were actually born on the same day, to parents who were best friends. We were raised together, but our bond is more than that.

We've known since we were teenagers that we were destined to share a mate. I never wanted to be away from him, and he felt the same way. We've gone out looking for our mate with that in mind. Hell, we designed our house with that in mind, but now that big bed in the master bedroom is starting to just be a hurtful reminder.

"Smells like snow," Liam comments, pulling me out of my thoughts, and I let my bear sniff the air.

"Probably not today."

"Tonight," he says, and I nod.

Snow is just a common occurrence in Aspen Ridge, Alaska. The few humans that are in town are probably stocking up or already bundled up inside their homes, but us shifters aren't too worried by it. Some of our animals even prefer the snow, but that's mainly the polar bears who live north of town.

We both pick up the pace, wanting to get our groceries and get back to our house. A familiar shape comes into view on the trail, and I grin when I spot Ryder. My bear pouts when he sees that he's with his mate, but I ignore him and try to bury the jealousy that I feel for my friend as I wave my hand at him.

"Hey, Ryder. Hey, Sienna," I greet them, and Liam does the same.

"Hey, guys. Are you getting your groceries too?" Sienna asks as she swings the plastic bag in her hand slightly.

Ryder is glaring at the bag, his arms overloaded with

more groceries, and I'm sure he's upset that he's not carrying all of them.

Shifters are naturally overprotective of our mates. We want to spoil each other and take care of one another. If Liam and I had our mate, we wouldn't let her lift a finger.

"Yeah, we just need a few things," I tell them, and they nod.

Sienna is smiling, her camera hanging around her neck, and I wonder if she was out taking photos. She's a wildlife photographer who was only in town for an assignment, but then Ryder found her, and now Aspen Ridge is her home base.

She grins up at Ryder, and my heart drops.

Damn, I wish I could have that.

I frown. Those thoughts have been getting more and more frequent the last few weeks, and I don't know why. Is it just wintertime blues? Is it jealousy that our closest friend is mated and settled?

My bear starts to pace in agitation inside of me, and I force a smile to my lips.

"We'll see you guys later," I promise them, and Sienna waves as we pass them on the trail.

I glance back over my shoulder, my stomach clenching with envy when I see the way that Sienna and Ryder are smiling up at each other. You can see the love and respect between them, and my bear howls.

"I know," Liam whispers, and I glance at him.

He's trying to hide it, but I know him better than most. He looks just as envious and miserable as I feel right now.

"Maybe we should start looking again," I say gently, and I see his jaw clench.

He doesn't say anything back, and we finish our walk

into town in silence. The wind is starting to pick up, whipping snow and a few raindrops into our faces.

The Aspen Ridge Pack is one of the biggest in the world. It's divided into four sections; North, East, South, and West. Liam, Ryder, and I all live in the west section. It's where most of the bear shifters are because it's closest to the stream. Ryder is one of the only wolf shifters who have made this part their home.

There's a different Alpha for each section, but Liam and I live in a remote section, and since we don't cause any trouble, we don't see our Alpha all that much.

At the center of the pack land is the town. It's where the few tourists we get stay and where all the shops are. We head straight for the market, and I'm relieved to see that it's mostly empty.

Liam grabs a cart, and I walk beside him as we grab what we need. He remembers the garlic, and I smile as he tosses some into the cart.

"Are you making lasagna tonight?" He asks, and I nod.

"Yeah, I was talking to my mom last night, and she mentioned it. Now it's got me hungry for it too."

"How's she doing?" He asks me, that worried look in his eyes.

"Alright. She's comfortable, at least," I say, and he nods.

My mom has been sick for a while. She's been in and out of hospitals more and more lately, and the doctors have told us that the prognosis doesn't look good.

I know that her dream is to see me and Liam settled and mated before she passes. It's one of the reasons why Liam and I have been searching so hard. I know that she's just as disappointed as we are that we haven't found her yet.

"We'll have to go visit next week," Liam says, and I nod.

My parents and his live in Anchorage. They have better

doctors there so it made sense. Liam and I try to get out there once or twice a month for a visit, and we didn't get to go last month because of the snow storms so we're due a trip.

Liam pushes the cart toward the checkout, and I sigh as I follow after him.

I wish that we could break out of this funk.

TWO

Rue

THE AIR SMELLS FRESHER HERE in Aspen Ridge, but that's probably just my imagination. I imagine that the air would smell fresher, and I would feel lighter wherever I went, as long as my father wasn't there.

Today is my first official day of freedom. I spent all of last night on a bus with stiff, lumpy seats, but it was worth it to finally be away from my father and that house.

Now that I'm here though, I have a new set of problems. Namely, I need to find a job and a place to live, and fast.

I look at the slightly crumpled newspaper in front of me, scanning the listing of jobs. There aren't many, and the few that are listed I'm not in any way qualified for.

I sigh, switching over to the apartment and house listings. It's just as sparse as the job ones, and I can't help but wince when I see the prices listed there.

I chose to come to Aspen Ridge because it was a small town. I thought that it would be cheap, but I also thought that my father would never come looking for me here. I'm not sure he'll bother looking for me at all, but I wanted to be safe, just in case.

I wasn't allowed to use the computer or have a phone when living with my father, so the only research I could do about the area was limited. I had seen some job listings for Aspen Ridge a few weeks ago, and I thought I would be good.

I have some savings left after buying my bus ticket and a cheap disposable phone, but that's not much. I wasn't allowed to work, one of my father's many rules, and I was rarely given money for birthdays or holidays. All that I have is what I was able to scrape together from tutoring a few kids during lunch and the money that my best friend, Iggy, and her parents gave me.

Iggy and her family are the only ones who know how bad my home life was. She was the only one I told about how my father treated me.

It's always been just my dad and me. My mom died in childbirth, and my father has resented me for it ever since. He would constantly tell me that I had killed my mother and that I was worthless and nothing but a burden on him.

If he wasn't yelling at me, then he was ignoring me. He would lock me in a closet if he wanted to go away for the weekend, and when I learned how to pick the closet lock, he started throwing me in the basement.

I've been planning my escape since I was ten, but I didn't have the opportunity until I turned eighteen. I knew that I would need a high school diploma; luckily, I gradu-ated just last week. Yesterday was my birthday, and I cele-brated it with Iggy and her family before they drove me to the bus station.

I wonder if my dad has called them asking about me. I hope that he didn't cause them any trouble.

I wish Iggy could have come with me, but I could barely afford my bus ticket. She has a job, though, and she's already promised to come see me once I'm settled.

Iggy is my only friend. I was always so shy and afraid of my own shadow. I was an easy target for the bullies, but Iggy always had my back. I don't know what made her sit next to me that first day of school, but I'm so glad she did.

My heart kicks against my ribs as I think about how alone I am. It's what I wanted, sure, but it still stings. I've been alone my whole life, and deep down, I know it's not really what I want. I don't want to be alone; I just want to be able to be free.

I glance around the small downtown area of Aspen Ridge and wonder what I should do now. I don't have enough money to buy another bus ticket and start over somewhere new.

A cute little clothing store catches my eye, and I decide to start going into shops to see if anyone is hiring. I'm about to cross the road when my phone rings. It takes me a second to realize what it is. I'm still not used to having a cell phone.

The only person who has my number is Iggy, though, and I scramble to answer it.

"Are you okay?" I ask as soon as the call has connected.

"Funny, I was about to ask you the same thing," she says, and I let out a sigh of relief.

"I'm fine; I just, with my dad, I wasn't sure..." I say.

"I know," she says gently. "He never called. We drove by your house this morning, and things seemed quiet there."

I let out a breath of relief. At least he's not after me.

"How's Aspen Ridge?" Iggy asks.

"It's pretty," I tell her, and she pauses.

"And? How's the job search going? Where are you stay-ing?" She asks, rattling off questions.

"Slow. I'm out looking for a job right now, actually. I'll figure out where I'm staying this afternoon."

"Be careful. I checked the weather, and you're supposed to get snow in that area tonight."

Great. Now I need to worry about freezing to death on top of everything else...

I wish that Iggy was here with me. She could always make me smile and make me feel better. She had offered to let me stay with her and her family, but they were barely scraping by, and I know they couldn't afford another mouth to feed. Besides, I wanted to get out of our hometown and away from my father.

"Well, I'm already making plans to come out and see you! I asked for a week off next month from work. I'll text you once it's been approved."

"I can't wait to see you," I say honestly, and I can picture her smiling at my words.

"I know you don't have that many minutes so I'll let you go back to your job hunt. I'll talk to you soon!" She says, and I smile sadly.

"Love you."

"Love you more!"

She hangs up, and I swallow hard.

Talking to Iggy was great, but it's also a strong reminder that I'm screwed. Now I need to find a job and a place to stay more than ever.

I look up at the darkening sky and blow out a deep breath.

Please, let me find something to fix all of these problems fast.

THREE

Liam

I CAN SENSE Bo's sadness like it's my own, and it only further causes the wound inside me to stretch wider. I hate that he's been so down lately. His easygoing, upbeat mood has soured over the last few years as we searched for our mate and came up empty.

We've been all over the world looking for her, traveling since we turned eighteen, and were able to find our mate, but we still haven't found her. Haven't even caught a whiff of her scent.

My bear growls inside of me at the thought, and I absent-mindedly rub my chest as we check out at the market. Bo grabs his wallet, and I start loading the cart with the few bags of groceries.

My bear sags inside of me glumly as I think about what I'm going to do for the rest of the day. Bo and I are investors. We learned it from our parents, and we've been working together to build our small bank account into what it is today.

I do the research and pick which stocks or mutual funds we should invest in, and Bo handles the actual investing and our accounting. We've built it over the last five years and now, we'll never have to work another day in our lives. We could more than take care of our mate.

If only we could find her...

I push the cart back with the others, and Bo and I each take two bags. He follows me outside, and as soon as we step outside, we smell it.

"Our mate," Bo and I say at the same time.

We share an excited grin before we take off down the street. My bear is trying to break free, and I'm sure that Bo's is too, but we both know that there are humans around so we can't shift or bite our mate. Not here, anyway.

"We finally found her," Bo says, his voice bursting with happiness.

"I know."

We continue to speed walk down the sidewalk, both of our heads turning as we scan the street to try to find her. I take a deep breath, breathing in her sweet scent.

I can feel Bo's excitement coming off him in waves, and I grin. We're both over the moon excited that we've finally found her. My bear is spinning in circles inside me, his tongue practically wagging.

We're almost to the other side of town when we see her. There aren't that many people on the streets right now so it's easy to track her.

We both freeze in our tracks when we catch sight of her. Her red hair is braided down her back, but a few strands have come loose. She's leaning back against the brick wall of the bank; her arm crossed over her torso as she talks on the phone.

Her curvy body is dressed in a thick black sweater and a pair of jeans that look worn. She's wearing tennis shoes, and I frown. Those aren't nearly warm enough.

"We need to buy her warmer clothes," Bo says, reading my mind.

"I'll order her some as soon as we get back home," I tell him, and he nods.

As soon as she's off the phone, we're moving toward her. She's looking down at some papers in her hand, and I squint to make them out as we approach her. It isn't until we're a few feet away that we realize something.

She's human.

We share a look then, coming to an agreement to take things slow with her without saying a word.

"Are you lost?" I call out when we're only a couple of feet away.

Her head snaps up, and her blue eyes take us in.

"No, no, I was just looking for something."

"Us too," Bo whispers under his breath, and I bite back a smile.

"Looking for anything in particular?" I ask her.

"Um, a job," she says with a self-conscious laugh.

"I don't think anything in town is hiring," Bo says apologetically.

I know without looking that he wants to tell her that she never has to work a day in her life. That she never has to worry about anything again.

She seems wary of us, though. I can see it in the tension in her shoulders, the way that her eyes have that distrusting look in them. She shifts on her feet, and my bear whines. He wants her to want us too.

We would never hurt her, but we can't exactly come right out and say that. Why would she believe us anyway?

This might be harder than we thought it would be...

Now we'll have to explain shifters and fated mates instead of just biting and claiming her. With her not fully trusting us, that might take some time, but we've waited years to find her. A little longer won't kill us.

Probably.

I share a look with Bo and see that we're on the same page.

"I'm Liam, and this is Bo. What's your name, sweetheart?" I ask her, and she hesitates for the briefest of a second.

"Rue," she says quietly.

"That's a lovely name," I comment, and Bo nods, smiling wide at our pretty mate.

"Did you just get into town?" Bo asks.

It's obvious that she's new to town. We would have smelled her before now otherwise. I'm glad that he asked, though. We want to know everything about her.

"Yeah, this morning."

I can see that she has a job listing and rental listing in her hand, and I start to get an idea.

"Well, we're looking to hire a live-in housekeeper," I lie. "Do you have any experience with cooking or cleaning?"

Bo doesn't look surprised by my offering her a job. He was probably about to say the same thing.

Now we just need to convince her to take it. I mean, it's a win-win for everyone involved. She gets a job and a safe place to stay, and we get more time to win her over.

She perks up at my words, and my bear growls inside of me.

"I do. Do you have any other details?"

"It would be full-time. We can show you our house, and you're free to pick any room that you'd like. You'd have to clean and cook breakfast, lunch, and dinner," I lie.

Bo and I are both neat freaks, and I know we both plan on cooking for her and spoiling the shit out of her. She won't have much to do.

"What does it pay?" She asks and I can see the desperation in her eyes.

My stomach sinks as I wonder what this girl has been through.

"Five thousand a week," Bo says, and I want to hit him.

Her eyes widen, and that distrustful look is back.

"A month," I clarify. "Five thousand a month."

She relaxes slightly at that, but she still seems skeptical about us.

"Why don't we show you the house, and we can negotiate salary if you think that five thousand isn't enough," Bo says, and I nod.

She looks around, taking in the mostly deserted street. I can see that she knows she doesn't have any other options and takes a deep breath.

"Alright. Lead the way."

Bo and I share one last look, our bears both starting to pace inside of us as we start the walk back to our cabin.

FOUR

Bo

HAVING our mate in our house finally makes it feel like a home. Liam and I are both watching Rue take in our home like the predators that we are. We're tracking her every move, cataloging her facial expressions as she looks around so we know what she likes and doesn't like.

"You have a lovely home," Rue says, and I relax slightly.

"Thanks. Let me show you around," I say as Liam carries the groceries into the kitchen.

Rue nods, tightening her hold on her backpack. She seems a little uneasy being alone with us, and I can't help but wonder if something happened to her. If anyone dared to hurt our mate, Liam and I will rip their throats out.

"This is the living room, and down that hallway is the kitchen and a bathroom," I say, and Rue nods, her blue eyes wide as she tries to take everything in.

Liam comes out of the kitchen, and we head over to the stairs.

"There's an office and den over here," I tell her, motioning to the rooms on the other side of the stairs.

"Do you work from home?" Rue asks, and Liam nods.

"Yeah, we're investors," he tells her.

I lead us up the stairs to show Rue the bedrooms. I know that Liam and I are both hoping that Rue will pick the big bedroom. It's the one that we built and designed to share with our mate. It's been empty for the last five years. We both agreed that sleeping in there didn't feel right without our fated mate.

"Here's the first guest room," I lie.

The room is actually for our future children, but I don't want to tell Rue that. I'm not sure that she would take it well.

Rue pokes her head into the first guest room, and Liam and I both hold our breaths.

"There's also another one at the end of the hall," Liam says, and I nod, leading her over to the big bedroom.

Liam opens the door, and I watch Rue's face as she takes in the space.

"This is a guest room?" She blurts out, her eyes widening in surprise. "How big are your rooms?"

I smile, sidestepping the question. Liam and I both have rooms similar to the first guest room, but I'll keep that to myself.

"I'm guessing this is the one that you'd like then," Liam says, obviously trying to change the subject of our rooms too.

Rue nods, taking a step into the room and my bear rises to his feet inside of me. He was content to lie down as soon as Rue stepped into the house, but now, I can feel his patience is starting to wear thin. He wants to claim his mate.

He wants to see her walking around with our bite marks on her neck.

I have to agree with him. It feels so right to have her in our space. I know that we need to take things slowly but having her here, in this room, is starting to make me feel antsy.

"So, you would need to clean the house and then make a few meals. Bo and I can run any errands ourselves," Liam says, and I blink out of my fantasy of tackling her onto that bed and making her mine and try to focus.

"Right," I add lamely, my voice coming out gravely and making me sound like the beast that I am.

"Can I get you anything to drink, and we can sit down to talk salary?" Liam asks, shooting me a warning look.

"Sure," Rue says, looking between the two of us.

She can tell that we're having a silent conversation, but she doesn't know what about.

I turn, leading the way back downstairs and into the kitchen. Liam heads for the fridge and looks inside.

"How about some hot chocolate?" He asks when the wind picks up, rattling the windows.

"That would be great, thanks."

Rue takes a seat at the kitchen table, and I notice that she sets her backpack between her feet. One hand is still clinging to the strap, and it hits me then that all of her belongings must be inside that bag.

My bear snarls at the thought. Our mate should have the finest of everything. She shouldn't be worried about a few possessions.

I grit my teeth, holding him back as he stalks back and forth inside of me.

I take the seat next to Rue as Liam finishes making her hot chocolate. I want to tell her about shifters right now, but

I know it's not time. The words are there, though, on the tip of my tongue.

I swallow them back and instead ask, "How are you liking Aspen Ridge so far?"

"Well, I've really only been here for a few hours, but it seems like a nice town."

"Where are you from originally?" Liam asks as he passes her the hot chocolate and takes a seat on the other side of her.

"Anchorage," she answers, and I can see Liam stiffen in his seat.

She's been so close all this time. We've been in Anchorage over the last few months to see my mom, too, and we never knew she was there.

She must have just turned eighteen then. Otherwise, we would have been able to smell her before all of this.

"So, you're not too far from home then," Liam says, and I nod.

"Not yet," she mumbles, and I frown at Liam, wondering what that means.

I can see that Liam wants to ask her, too, but she interrupts us before we can.

"What brought you two to Aspen Ridge?" She asks.

My bear is pacing back and forth inside me, and I clench my hands into fists, begging him to calm down.

It's a losing battle, though. We've been dreaming about our mate for too long. We've wanted her for too long, and now that she's finally here, we can't hold back any longer.

"The pack," I say without really thinking, and Liam shoots me a look.

He's staring at me wide-eyed, silently warning me not to do this, but I can't stop. Not now that I've started.

"The pack?" She asks, taking a sip of her hot chocolate, and I nod.

"We're shifters," I tell her. "Bear shifters, though there are wolf and other animal shifters here."

The hot chocolate lands back on the table with a thump, some of the hot liquid splashing over the rim as Rue stares at me like I'm insane.

"Sorry, I didn't sleep very well last night. What did you say?" She asks, and I know that this is my chance to tell her that I was joking or pull it back, but I can't. I can't lie to her.

I can't hold myself back any longer. It's been so long, and we finally have her, so even though I know I'll probably regret it, I still can't help but tell her.

"Liam and I are bear shifters. And you're our fated mate."

FIVE

Rue

OH MY GOD, *these guys are crazy.*

Like certifiably insane.

I should have known that something was off when they just happened to run into me on the street with a job that paid a crazy amount of money.

It was too good to be true, but I let my heart take the lead for once instead of my head, and now I'm stuck way out in the middle of nowhere with these two big, hot men.

They're crazy, Rue! Don't get sucked in by their good looks!

I try to keep that in mind, but it's hard when I'm staring at them. Both men have dark hair, though Liam's is a little lighter though, more dark brown than black. Their eye color is the only thing that seems to be really different. Bo has blue eyes, whereas Liam has green. I can't decide which color I like better.

Liam is shooting daggers at Bo right now, and I look

between the two men, wondering what the hell I should do now. My fingers tighten on my backpack, and I push to my feet.

"I don't think I'll be taking the job," I say, bolting for the door, but their faster.

I don't even know how it's possible for them to move so fast. They're both well over six feet tall and thick as oak trees. Yet, they both make it to the front door before me.

"You can't leave," Bo says.

"Not yet. Please, just let us explain," Liam pleads.

"I really need to get going," I say, looking around for another exit.

"You can't leave," Bo repeats, and I glare at him.

"Are you two really going to force me to stay here?" I snap, and they both nod in unison.

"Please, just hear us out," Liam tries again.

I can't, though. There's just something about seeing them standing in my way, forcing me to do what they want, trapping me here that reminds me of my father, and I snap.

I can't believe that I'm being held captive once again. I just escaped one controlling asshole and thought things would be better. Instead, I traded one man for two.

Tears sting the back of my eyes, and I blink rapidly. I always do this. Crying whenever I get mad or upset, and I hate that they're seeing me when I look so weak.

"Rue, no," Bo whispers, coming toward me in an instant.

The next thing I know, both men are wrapped around me, practically smothering me as they hold me close.

"Please don't cry, sweetheart," Liam begs, and I sniffle into his shirt.

It hits me then that maybe these men aren't entirely like my father. My dad used to hate it when I cried. He never once comforted me. Instead, he would mock me until I realized it was better to cry when I was alone. Sometimes though, I just couldn't help it.

Bo and Liam both seem to hate seeing me upset, though. They didn't hesitate to try to comfort me. My father wouldn't have cared about my tears, but these two men can't seem to stand seeing me cry.

"We'll fix this," Bo promises.

"You just have to let us explain everything," Liam adds.

I take a deep breath, wiping the tears from my eyes, and nod.

"Fine. You have five minutes," I say, trying to sound tough and confident.

The men lead me over to the leather couch, and I sink into the soft cushion. They both take seats in the chairs across from me, looking nervous and on edge.

"We're really bear shifters," Liam starts, and Bo nods.

"We're part of the Aspen Ridge Pack," Bo adds.

"Okay..." I say.

"Shifters can change from human to their animal form at will, but we keep that hidden from humans. There have been too many instances over history where humans try to kill our kind or lock us up to do experiments on us," Liam continues, and my heart breaks.

I hate the thought of anyone being locked up.

"We have heightened senses and healing powers. Different animal shifters can do different things, but we all have a better sense of smell and sight than the average human," Liam says.

"Shifters each have a fated mate, someone they were destined to be with. Shifters won't ever love or be with anyone else but their mate."

"And you are ours," Bo finishes.

"How do you know that?" I ask, my curiosity getting the better of me.

"We can smell you," Liam says.

"You smell like cotton candy and strawberries," Bo says, licking his lips, and my core clenches at the action.

I don't know why they're doing this, but I need to get out of here. I glance back at the door, and I hear both men shift in their seats.

"Okay, prove it," I tell them, and they share a look.

Maybe I can escape while they're changing into their animals...

"Okay," Liam says, and I pause.

I half expected my challenge to be calling their bluff. Now I'm not sure what to make of all of this.

They stand and start taking off their shirts, and I frown. That was definitely not what I was expecting, and maybe I should look away, but I can't seem to tear my eyes away from them. Especially not when all of their tanned skin and muscles come into view.

Hair covers their chests with a trail leading down to the waistbands of their jeans and my mouth starts to water at the sight of both of them. They toe off their boots, but I don't pay attention to that. I'm too busy watching the way their muscles shift and contract with each movement.

When their hands reach for the buttons on their jeans, I snap out of it and look away. My hand tightens on my backpack, and I take a deep breath.

Get it together, Rue! You need to get out of here.

"Ready?" Bo asks, and for a second, I think that maybe he read my thoughts, but I realize that they mean about them shifting.

I glance back at them, and both men have their hands on the waistbands of their jeans like they're ready to push them down. I nod my head, gripping my backpack tighter as my muscles tighten.

As soon as they bend down, I'm going to make a run for it.

"Ready," I say, and they nod.

I glance away when they pull their pants down, my heart racing as my muscle tighten, getting ready to run. Then a strange sound comes from by the fireplace, and I look over to see the two big men changing into bears.

My mouth drops open, and I stare in shock as two big grizzly bears stand before me.

"Holy shit," I whisper, and they nod their heads.

I stand, but I'm not sure if I'm going to run toward them or away. They make the choice for me, ambling my way until their soft fur brushes my hand.

"This can't be happening. I'm dreaming," I whisper, but even as I say the words, my hands are brushing along the bears' backs.

The bear with blue eyes grumbles happily as my fingers sink into his fur, and I know it's Bo. The green-eyed one nudges my hand, and I turn to him, giving him the same pets.

"Okay. So, you're not crazy," I say, my knees giving out as I sink back onto the couch.

Both men shift back, and I look away from them as they tug their pants back on. They open their mouths to say what, I don't know.

Suddenly, a loud boom sounds, and the whole house rattles. Both men are instantly by my side, and I stare wide-eyed out the front window as a wall of snow seems to rush by.

The noise goes on for what feels like minutes, and I

cling to Bo and Liam as we watch the snow start to climb up the window.

Then there's nothing but quiet.

All of us are breathing hard, and I turn to them.

"What the hell was that?" I ask, my voice shaking.

"An avalanche," Liam says grimly, and Bo nods.

They both look worried, and maybe I should be concerned about our food or water supply or staying alive until we can get out, but that's not what's on my mind. Instead, as I stare out the front window, all I can think is, great, now we're all trapped here.

SIX

Liam

THIS IS NOT how I imagined meeting my fated mate would go. I never anticipated that she would be human and that we would need to convince her to be with us, and I certainly never expected an avalanche to trap us in our house together. We never wanted to hold our mate captive. We want her to choose us too.

I doubt that will happen now...

I glance at Bo, and he looks just as clueless about what to do next as I am. Maybe the avalanche is a good thing. At the very least, it just bought us some time to try to win her over. All of this talk about shifters and mates probably just overwhelmed her.

She just needs time.

With my plan in place, I turn back to Rue.

"Are you hungry?" I ask, and she blinks at me, but her stomach growls. "I'll make dinner."

I grab my shirt off the coffee table and tug it over my

head, knowing without looking that Bo is doing the same. I turn to head back to the kitchen, and a second later, I hear Bo's footsteps trail after me.

"Um, what the hell are we going to do?" He whispers to me as soon as we're alone.

"We're going to make dinner and try to convince her that no one will love her more or treat her better than we will," I tell him calmly.

He doesn't look as confident in my plan, but he nods.

"What are we making?" He asks as I open the fridge to peer inside.

The sound of the front door opening catches both of our attentions, and we share one panicked look before we take off back to the living room.

The front door is wide open, and neither of us pauses as we take off after Rue. The wind is blowing snow and ice around outside, and it's almost waist-deep on us so I know that she couldn't have gotten far.

The snow freezes my feet, and I wince but don't slow down as we trek through the path after our mate. She's surprisingly fast, and we're a few feet away from the house before I spot her up ahead.

"No!" Bo shouts at the same time that I realize that she's about to walk off the side of the cliff.

She probably can't see it with all the snow flying around. but our house was built close to a cliff. It provides a great view of the mountains. Bo and I had talked about putting up a fence or something, but it seemed unnecessary. Now I'm wishing that we had.

"Rue! Stop!" I yell after her, picking up my pace.

My bear is tense and on his feet inside of me. He wants out, and he would probably be faster. I know that she's already seen us shift, but I'm worried that seeing two big grizzly bears chasing after her would only freak her out more. It's clear that she's overwhelmed right now with everything that has happened and I don't want to make it worse.

We're almost to her now, and the wind picks up, blowing her back away from the edge. She glances over her shoulder at us, her blue eyes squinting against the blowing snow. Bo and I both run faster, and she tries to push through the snow, but the adrenaline must be wearing off. She's tiring quickly, and that's the only thing that allows us to get to her in time.

I grab her wrist right as she takes a step off the cliff, and she screams as she slips down.

"I've got you," I tell her.

"We've got you," Bo says as he grabs her other hand, and we tug her back to safety.

"You shouldn't be out here dressed like that," I tell her, taking my shirt off and wrapping it around her.

Bo does the same, and then we're sandwiching her between us, using our bodies to block out most of the snow as we hustle back to the cabin.

"We need to get you by the fire," I say.

"I'll get a change of clothes. You can't be in that wet stuff," Bo says as he takes the stairs two at a time.

I set Rue down in front of the fire, adding a few logs to build the flames up more. It's already hot in the house, but after being out in that blizzard, she's going to need more heat if she's to warm up.

Bo comes jogging back downstairs with a change of clothes and two blankets in his arms. We don't say anything as we help Rue pull off her wet clothes and in to our dry ones. We work as a team, taking care of our mate and making sure that she has everything she needs.

This is what I always wanted. Being around Rue gives me a greater purpose than a job or hobby ever could. Taking care of her is what I'm meant to do with my life.

Bo disappears into the kitchen as I wrap Rue up in the blankets and set her down on the chair closest to the fireplace. She hasn't said a word, which makes me and my bear a bit uneasy, but at least she's back here and safe.

"Here, I made you some more hot chocolate," Bo says, passing her the steaming mug.

"Do you need anything else?" I ask her, and she shakes her head.

"You can't... you can't do that," Bo says, and I can hear how shaken up he is.

"Please, don't do that again," I say quietly, and she nods.

"Just give us some time.

"Until the weather clears," I add, and Bo nods.

"Let us try to show you that we're not crazy and that you're meant to be with us," he finishes.

She looks between us, her gaze sliding back to the window, and for a second, I'm worried that she will reject us.

"Alright," she says reluctantly.

I have a feeling that she's only saying that because of the weather, but I'll take it. We have a few days now, a few days to show her that we were destined to love her and take care of her.

I share a look with Bo, and he has a grim kind of determination in his eyes that I've never seen before. Normally he's the fun, easy-going one of the two of us, but when it comes to our mate, I guess this is the only thing he's willing to take seriously.

"We'll go finish dinner," I tell her, and she nods, sipping her hot chocolate.

Bo follows me down the hallway and back into the kitchen. As soon as we're alone, he blows out a deep breath.

"How are we going to win her over?" He asks me as he leans back against the kitchen counter.

"We're going to be the best goddamn mates that ever lived," I tell him, and he nods.

We get to work then, both of us silent as we try to come up with a new game plan.

SEVEN

Bo

I WAKE up the next day with a smile on my face. I can smell Rue, can hear her gentle breathing coming from next door, and my bear is finally at peace inside of me.

Well, maybe not at peace, but he's happy. He'd be a lot happier, though, if we were in bed with our mate.

I barely slept last night. I was too wired after everything that happened yesterday. I spent way too long last night lying in bed and listening to Rue move around next door. I was trying to come up with a way to win her over, to show her that she can trust us and that all we want to do is love her.

I didn't come up with anything concrete. I figure if we just spoil her and show her everything that we can give her; maybe she'll come around.

I get up to take a shower, and I can hear Liam climbing out of bed too. I strip and hop in the shower. My plan is to surprise Rue with breakfast in bed. We can't leave the house so nice dates are out, but there's still things that we can do together here.

I hurry through my morning routine and tug on some clean clothes. When I step out of the bedroom, I notice that Rue's bedroom door is already open. For a moment, my anxiety spikes. What if she tried to leave again?

I sprint down the stairs, checking the front door, but it's still locked. Clanging comes from the kitchen, and I head in that direction.

My bear and I both relax as we see Rue moving around the kitchen.

"Sorry, did I wake you?" She asks, her cheeks turning a pale pink as she sets the pan down on the stove.

"No, I was headed down to make you breakfast in bed, actually," I tell her.

"In bed?" she asks like she's never heard of it.

"Yeah, have you never eaten in bed?" I ask her as I start the coffee pot.

"No, that wasn't allowed at my house."

The way she says it has my bear and I both standing at attention. She sounds so sad, so small, and I hate it.

"Why don't you go back to bed, and you can try it today?" I offer.

"No, I want to help around here. I can cook."

I nod, smiling as Liam comes into the kitchen, still rubbing the sleep from his eyes.

"Morning," he says, dropping a kiss on the top of Rue's head as he walks to the coffee pot.

I stare at him, wondering if he even realized what he just did. He made it look so casual, and I'm sure he did it without thinking.

Rue is staring at him; her mouth opens slightly, but when he doesn't react, she just blinks and turns away.

"Morning," I say.

"Are we making breakfast?" He asks after he takes a sip of his coffee.

"We were just about to," I tell him, and he nods.

He sets his coffee cup down and moves over to Rue, picking her up and setting her down on the counter like she weighs nothing. She squeaks, looking at him with wide eyes. Her hands are gripping his shoulders, and I see his hands tighten on her hips.

"I was going to take things slow with you, but we don't have that much time so I can't tiptoe around. For the next few days, Bo and I are going to show you what it would be like to be ours," he tells her, and she opens her mouth, but no words come out.

I like his plan a lot more than mine, and I grin.

"You look beautiful this morning, baby," I tell her, and she glances at me.

"Thanks," she mumbles after a beat, her cheeks turning almost as red as her hair.

"Rue has never had breakfast in bed," I tell Liam, and he smiles at me.

"We'll have to fix that," he says, and she eyes him warily, but I can see the hint of excitement in her blue eyes too.

"I'm helping cook," she tells him firmly, and he nods.

"Fine. Then we all eat in bed."

He drops a quick kiss on her lips before he moves to the fridge, and I follow his lead, stepping between her spread thighs and cupping her face in my hands. I dip my head, brushing my lips against hers in a barely there kiss before I pull back.

"Thank you," I whisper, and she frowns.

"For what?"

"For giving us a chance. For being here."

She nods, seeming to soften slightly.

Liam is already getting started making pancakes and bacon. Without saying anything to each other, we both seem to agree to steal as many touches or soft kisses as we can as we cook. My bear is curled up inside of me, loving that we're so close to her. By the time the food is done, we have Rue's scent all over us, and my bear and I couldn't be more content.

"I'll get the food," I volunteer, and Liam nods.

"I'll grab the drinks," he says.

"What should I carry up?" Rue asks as she looks around.

"Just yourself, baby," I tell her, and she blushes but nods.

I wish I could peel that snug shirt off of her and see how far down that blush goes, but it's not time for that. I only hope that by the mating moon tomorrow night, she trusts us a little more. It seems like too much to hope that she could want us by then.

We follow Rue upstairs and into the master bedroom. As soon as she crawls onto the bed, I know I want to do this every day for the rest of my life.

"It's like a little indoor picnic," I say as we spread the food out on the comforter and place the glasses on the bedside tables.

"I've never been on one of those either," Rue admits, and my heart breaks at the sad tone of her voice.

She looks so excited to be getting to do it now, though, and I know that Liam and I will be trying to offer her any experience that she wants from now on.

"You and your mom never had tea parties when you were younger?" Liam asks, and she shakes her head.

"No, my mom died during childbirth with me," she says as she starts to fill her plate with pancakes and bacon.

Liam and I share a look, and I can see the sadness in his eyes. I wish our mate had never known such heartbreak, and I hate that I can't change anything.

"We never had tea parties with our moms either," I say. "But we did bake cookies, cuddle for movies, and play board games when we were younger."

"We could do that together today," Liam offers.

"You guys want to be my mom?" Rue asks in confusion, and Liam almost spits out his coffee.

"No," I say.

"Definitely not," Liam adds.

"We just want you to have those experiences. I get the feeling that maybe you haven't had many of them, and since we can't leave the house right now, this is the best we can do. Once the snow melts, we can do whatever you want," I promise her.

She nods, her eyes looking a little glassy, but she looks away before I can tell if I've upset her or not.

We all start eating, and Liam and I share a few looks throughout breakfast. I can tell that we're both trying to gauge how the other thinks things are going, but it's hard to tell with Rue. She plays her cards close to her chest.

"You were born here?" Rue asks after a few minutes, and we nod.

"Yep. Our parents were best friends. We were actually born on the same day and pretty much raised together," I tell her.

"We've traveled, though," Liam adds. "We've been all over the world the last five years looking for you."

"For me?"

"For our mate. We've been to Anchorage, too, but we can't smell you until you're eighteen. That must have been recently," I say, and she nods.

"Two days ago."

"If you hadn't come here, we would have found you next week when we visit my mom," I tell her.

"Your parents don't still live here?"

"No, my mom is sick. Her doctors are in Anchorage, so our parents made the move out there last year," I tell her.

"Bo, I'm so sorry," she says, and I nod.

"She's a fighter. She could still pull through," Liam says, resting his hand on my shoulder in support.

I change the subject to a happier topic. I only have a few precious days with Rue, and I don't want her to be sad during any of them.

"What kind of cookies should we make today?" I ask them, and Liam smiles.

"Chocolate chip, obviously," he says, and I shake my head.

"S'mores," I argue, and we turn to Rue to decide.

"Both," she says with a shy smile, and I grin.

"See! You are perfect for us," I say before I lean over and smack a kiss against her lips.

She laughs, seeming to have grown used to the physical affection and contact from us already. That has to be a good sign.

"We'll clean up the dishes. Why don't you take a shower or relax for a bit," Liam suggests, and Rue nods.

"We'll come get you when we're ready to start making cookies."

"Okay," Rue says as we gather up the dishes and head for the door.

We hear the shower kick on as we dump the plates and silverware in the sink, and I smile to myself as we get to work cleaning everything up.

"She's perfect, man," I tell Liam, and he nods.

He's humming under his breath as we work to wipe down the counters and do the dishes. We're just laying out the flour and sugar when Rue comes into the kitchen. Her hair is still a little damp from her shower, and her skin is a rosy pink that has my cock hardening in my pants.

My bear sits up inside of me, licking his lips at the sight of our curvy little mate.

"Ready to bake some cookies?" Liam asks, and Rue nods excitedly.

We spend the day talking and laughing together as we bake cookies. We cuddle on the couch, the fire crackling as we watch a few episodes of New Girl. It's Rue's favorite show, and I try to pay attention to it for her, but all I can focus on is all of the places where her body touches mine.

After dinner, Liam drags out a few board games, and we learn that Rue is a master at Clue and Candy Land. We let Rue pick a game, and she laughed when she found Pretty, Pretty, Princess. I don't even know why we have that game or where we got it, but I don't care. It was incredible to see Rue laughing so much when Liam ended up winning. The little plastic crown barely fit on his head, but he made it work, and it made our girl so happy.

Rue even let us kiss her goodnight before we all went to our own rooms. She seems a lot more comfortable around us now, and I know that Liam and I are both thinking the same thing.

Tomorrow we need to ramp things up another notch.

I can't wait to see how tomorrow goes, especially with the mating moon.

It was a perfect day, and as I crawl into bed and close my eyes, all I can think is that I can't wait to do it again every day for the rest of our lives.

EIGHT

Rue

WHEN ALL OF THIS STARTED, I was so sure that I would be walking out of here, away from these men, and that I would never think about them again. It's been two days, though, and already, I can't imagine ever being able to forget about Bo and Liam.

These last few days have been so magical. I never thought that I would have anything close to this in my life. I had resigned myself to being alone or just with Iggy. I thought I could be happy that way, and maybe I could have, but that was before I met my boys.

I've never even been interested in a man before. I was too busy trying to make it through school and save up money to really pay them much attention, but still. No one ever caught my eye. It seems crazy that I went from not looking twice at a man to having such strong feelings for two of them at once.

Bo and Liam keep talking about how I'm meant to be

with both of them, and they say it so casually like it's completely normal. I wonder if shifters usually share mates. Humans don't, though, and I wonder if something is wrong with me. How can I want to be with two men at the same time?

I wish that I could talk to Iggy about all of this. She would be able to help me talk this out. I tried calling her yesterday but couldn't get any service here. I'm not sure if it's because of the snow or maybe we're just too far from town to get cell service here.

I sigh, rolling over in the big bed. This thing is the most comfortable mattress that I've ever slept on. I'm not surprised. Everything with Bo and Liam seems to be perfect.

We had the best day yesterday. They were so sweet and attentive, but can I really trust that? What if this is all an act?

My dad must have been sweet to my mom, too, at one point at least, but that sure changed. What's stopping Liam and Bo from changing too?

Doubts start to fill my head, and I hate it. I want to go back to where I was when I first woke up. I was so excited to see what we were going to do today.

I throw the covers off of me, scooting all the way over to the side of the bed. I swear this bed is the size of a football field, and I wonder why it's in the guest room.

I head into the shower, taking time to get ready for the day as I try to think about what I should do.

I can't deny that I'm attracted to both of them, but I'm a virgin. Am I really ready to take on two men?

Do I want something long-term? I was supposed to be gaining some independence and building a new life. Can I really do that with Bo and Liam around? They barely even let me cook breakfast with them yesterday. They'll never let me stand on my own two feet.

I sigh, turning the water off and wrapping myself in a fluffy towel. I can hear my phone ringing as soon as the water is off, but it takes me a second to realize that it's mine.

I bolt into the bedroom, answering the call on the last ring.

"Iggy," I say, and she huffs.

"Are you okay? I tried to call you yesterday, but the call wasn't going through! I saw that there was a bad storm in Aspen Ridge, and I've been so worried," she says.

"I'm okay; I'm safe," I promise her, and she lets out another huff.

I can hear the stress and worry in her voice, and I'm sure that she's been freaking out all day. I should have asked the boys if I could borrow their computer. I could have at least sent her an email to let her know I was okay.

"Where are you?"

"At..." I start, but I don't know how to finish that sentence.

What do I say? That I'm at work? It would be a lie since I never took the job.

At my boyfriends' place?

Well, I have to tell her sometime.

"I met these two guys," I blurt out, and silence greets me. "Iggy?"

"Tell. Me. Everything," she squeals, and I can't help but laugh.

"Their names are Bo and Liam. They took me in when it was starting to snow," I half lie.

"And?" She asks, drawing the word out.

"And they're really hot," I admit, and she squeals again.

"Have you tried to jump their bones yet?" She asks, and I laugh.

"No, but they've kissed me and stuff."

"What's the and stuff?" She pries.

"Cuddles, hand holding. PG-rated stuff."

"Oh," she says with a disappointed sigh.

"You were hoping that it was blow jobs and foreplay?" I ask with a laugh.

"Uh, yeah! You're only young once, babe! Live!"

Maybe Iggy is right. I've spent my entire life until now following the rules and all alone. Maybe it's time that I had a bit of fun.

I know that Bo and Liam will take care of me. I know that they will make sure that my first time is perfect. So why am I holding back?

I want to tell Iggy about shifters and them sayingI was their fated mate, but something holds me back. Maybe it's because of what the boys said. They have to trust the people that they tell, and I trust Iggy explicitly, but I think that it should be a shifter's choice to share that with her.

"Okay," I say, and I think I shock both of us.

"Okay? You're going to do it?" She asks excitedly, and I nod.

"Yeah, I'm going to do it."

"Call me immediately after! I want all of the details! Try to take pictures!" She says, and I laugh.

"I won't be doing that, but I will call you," I promise.

"Party pooper," she teases, and I grin.

"I'll talk to you soon."

"Love you!"

"I love you too."

I end the call and collapse back onto the bed with a

wide smile stretching my face. I knew that Iggy would talk some sense into me.

Now I just need to be brave enough to go through with it.

I hurry to get dressed, pulling on my tightest pair of yoga pants and a t-shirt that's been washed so many times it's partially see-through. I don't really have the wardrobe to pull off seduction, but I have a feeling that it won't take much to convince Bo and Liam to take me to bed.

I head downstairs, following the scent of bacon and eggs into the kitchen. The boys are busy cooking what looks to be a feast, and I breathe in the scent of baked goods and sugar.

"It smells so good in here," I say, and they both turn to me with a smile that quickly transforms into a hungry look when they see what I'm wearing.

I ignore the darkening eyes and the way that they lick their lips as I head over to the kitchen table and grab a strawberry.

"Can I do anything?" I ask as I bite into the sweet fruit.

I look over at them innocently, and they're both staring at me. Lust is the only thing I see when I look into their faces; it has my heart racing and my panties growing damp.

I want these two men to take me. I want them to claim me.

"I think something is burning," I point out, and they curse quietly as they rush to pop the toast and finish cooking breakfast.

Bo and Liam both keep stealing glances at me, and I bite back a smile as I take a seat. I don't know if it's because I've decided to seduce them or what, but there's just something different today. Some strange kind of current between the three of us that I've never experienced before.

I feel so connected to them, and I wonder why that is. There's a heightened sense of arousal, and for the first time, I wonder if they can smell it on me.

"Oh my god!" I gasp, and they both whip around, ready to fix whatever has upset me.

"What?" Liam asks when he doesn't see anything that could have made me gasp like that.

"Can you two smell how turned on I am?" I blurt out.

Bo bends over, resting his head on the counter like he's in pain, and I stand, wanting to go to him.

"She's trying to kill us," Bo whispers, but I hear him.

Liam is just staring at me with wide eyes and a strained look on his face.

"I need a minute," he says, and Bo tries to grab him before he can leave, but he's too late.

"What's going on?" I ask Bo as I move closer to him.

"We promised not to do anything until after we talked with you," he says, and I nod.

"A talk about what?" I ask, still following him around the kitchen island.

"About mates and the mating moon."

"Okay, let's talk."

"Not right now," he half begs, and I pout.

He groans, closing his eyes.

"Please, baby. Don't do this. Not just yet," he begs, and I sigh.

"Fine, but answer my question," I say, and he blinks.

"Yeah," he says hoarsely. "We can smell when you're turned on."

"That doesn't seem fair," I murmur. "How will I know if you two are turned on?"

I walk closer, our chests brushing together now, and Bo stares down at me, a slightly tortured look on his face.

"Easy. If we're in the same room as you, we're turned on. We will always want you, Rue."

"Prove it," I whisper as I rise up onto my tiptoes.

My lips brush against his, and he lets out an agonized groan before his hands tangle in my hair, and he crushes me against him.

My fingers tangle in his black hair, and I close my eyes as I let Bo take the lead. His lips move over mine, his tongue licking along the seam of my lips, begging for entry.

I open for him, ready for him to do whatever he wants with me, but heavy footsteps sound in the hall and Bo pulls back.

"Not yet," he says, his voice low and gravely.

I don't get a chance to respond before he lifts me up and carries me over to the table. He drops me down onto a chair and pulls out the one next to me as Liam walks into the room.

My hand reaches up, stroking along my swollen lips, and I hear Bo groan next to me. The kiss felt different today. Maybe it's because it was more than a peck, or maybe it's because today, I initiated it. Either way, I can't wait for more.

I smile sweetly at Liam as I rest my hand on Bo's strong thigh, and when I hear Bo let out a muffled curse, I know that this is going to be fun.

NINE

Liam

SHE'S TRYING to kill us.

That's the only explanation I can think of for why Rue has done a complete one-eighty and is now trying to seduce us.

I mean, don't get me wrong, I love it. I just wish that Bo and I hadn't promised each other to take things slow with her today.

We need to tell her what it means to be mated and about the mating moon. I thought it would be a hard conversation, but now I'm wondering if maybe Rue can already feel the mating moon.

Lord knows that Bo and I can.

We both woke up with it already starting to press down on us. I didn't think that humans would be able to feel it, but maybe I was wrong. Maybe that's all this is, and our plan to win her over yesterday didn't work at all.

"We'll get that," I tell Rue as she starts to carry dishes over to the sink.

She shrugs, brushing against me as she heads to the living room to warm up by the fire, and I bite back a groan. My bear is begging me to bite her and claim her, but we need to be open and honest about what being our mate entails. We need to make sure that this is what she wants before we make her ours.

He growls, flashing his teeth at me, and I know he doesn't care about that. He just wants his mate.

"She kissed me," Bo hisses at me as he helps me carry over the dirty dishes.

I look at him sharply, hope growing inside of me. Most men would probably be jealous that their friend got kissed first, but I'm not worried about that. I'm just excited that it happened.

"That has to be a good sign, right?" I ask him, and he nods.

"I hope so. I just can't tell if she's doing it because she wants us..."

"Or if it's the mating moon," I finish, and he nods.

It's winter in Alaska, which means that the sun won't be out for too much longer. It's already after noon, and I know we need to talk with her before we're all too overcome with the mating heat to think clearly.

"Is there any dessert?" Rue asks, walking back into the room, and I share a look with Bo, both of us wondering what she's playing at.

I mean, who eats dessert after breakfast?

"Ice cream?" Bo offers, and I want to hit him.

I glare at him, and I can see the second he realizes how he messed up.

"That sounds great."

He goes to get her a bowl, and I take a seat next to her at the table, steeling myself and my bear for what's about to happen.

Bo passes her the bowl, and I stiffen as soon as she grabs her spoon. Just like at breakfast, as soon as she takes a bite, Bo and I are glued to her.

My cock hardens in my jeans as we watch her lips wrap around the spoon. She gives a happy little sigh as she takes a bite of ice cream, and I bite back a groan.

I look over at Bo and see his eyes are dark, filled with want. We barely survived her eating breakfast without pinning her to the floor and rutting into her like animals. Now he's given her ice cream.

Her pink tongue darts out, licking a stray drop of ice cream off of her spoon, and I grip the underside of the table as I feel my claws start to come out. I'm starting to lose my skin, and I'm too turned on to care all that much.

Stop! You're going to scare her off!

I grit my teeth, trying to get myself under control, but I can feel my claws still sinking into the wood, leaving deep grooves in their wake.

She shifts in her chair, and instantly, my bear and I are on high alert. We sit in silence as we watch her eat her ice cream, and by the time she's done, we're both sweating and grinding our teeth from holding ourselves and our bears back.

She sighs as she sets her bowl aside, and Bo frowns.

"Do you want more?" He asks, and I close my eyes in pain.

Please say no. I can't take much more of this.

"No, it's just... I can't take it anymore!" She blurts out, and I blink.

"What's wrong?" I ask her.

"I just need..."

"Need what?" Bo asks.

"Just say it, and it's yours," I promise her.

"I need you... both of you."

I glance at Bo, and we have a silent conversation.

We haven't told her about the mating moon and mates more yet; I remind him.

We can tell her later! She's obviously in need, he argues back.

I nod, and just like that, we're on her in a second.

TEN

Bo

CARRYING Rue into our bedroom is the greatest moment of my life. She's staring up at me with such trust and longing in her eyes, and I know that I'm never going to do anything to take that look away.

This girl was made for me and Liam, and now we're finally getting to make her ours in every way.

I lay her down on the bed, making sure that she's positioned in the middle of the bed. I know that Liam and I will need room to do all the things we want to do to her.

Thank God that we have this big bed...

Rue shifts self-consciously on the bed as Liam and I stand back and stare down at her.

"Relax, sweetheart. Let us take care of you," Liam coos at her, and she relaxes, nodding slightly.

I glance at the window, noticing that the sun is just now starting to set. It's still early, the mating moon isn't even out yet, but there's nowhere else that Liam and I want to be than in that bed with our mate.

We start to move at the same time, neither of us needing words, as we start to strip off our clothes. Rue watches us, her eyes wide and a dark blue now. They're filled with lust and longing, and I imagine Liam and I look similar.

I look over at him, and he nods, letting me know it's time to finally mark our mate. We both slip into the bed with her, and I move to wrap my arms around her waist. I smile when I feel her nuzzle her face into my neck. Her warm breath fans over my sensitive skin, and my cock hardens between our bodies.

Liam moves behind her, fitting his front to her back and wrapping his arm around her waist too before he buries his face in her shoulder. I can hear him breathing in her sweet scent. My bear breathes deeply, wanting to roll around in her scent. He's anxious inside me, wanting to sink his teeth into her neck and mark her.

Rue shifts between us, her curvy thighs opening, and my leg slips between them to keep them spread. My thick erection rubs against her soft curves, and I wish we were all naked already. When I hear Liam let out a groan, I know that he's just as turned on and probably wishing the same thing.

My fingers brush against her soft skin as I take in her delicate features. Her red hair looks like a blaze of fire, spread out across the pillow and around her shoulders. I feel her shift against us again, and I freeze, my hand gripping her hip when I hear her let out a sweet moan.

My eyes fly to Liam's, and I see him grinning as he watches her move against me. I've never seen him look so content and happy.

My bear is licking his lips as Rue continues to rock her

hips against me again and again, and the smile falls, replaced with a pained look when he realizes that we still have to mark her and convince her to be our mate.

Shifters can't come until they've marked their mate, and we haven't marked Rue yet. Feeling her rub against us will just be torture until we've bitten her. Liam looks at me, biting back a moan when she starts to move against us more forcefully. His blue eyes look pained, and I'm sure mine are the same, but we both know that we would never deny our mate anything.

If we bite her now, will she be thinking clearly enough to understand what we're asking of her? Maybe we should get her off first. We can clear her head and then ask her to be our mate and mark her.

My bear growl inside of me, hating that idea, but I want to make sure that Rue is on board with everything.

My cock slips between her legs, my bare skin rubbing against her thin yoga pants. I can feel her hard nipples through her shirt as they press into my chest, and I bite back a groan as she lets out a moan.

My bear is pacing inside of me, desperate to get out and claim our mate. I feel Liam's dick settle into the cleft of her ass, pulling the fabric of her yoga pants tighter against her and he bites down on his bottom lip as she moves against us. My eyes close tight when I hear her moan out our names.

Wetness spreads across the tip of my cock and I ease back so that Liam can push forward and feel her wetness against him as well. He curses under his breath when he feels the wet fabric against him, and I smile. He grins back at me, and we both cuddle her closer as she sighs between us.

"We're going to get you off, baby. Then we need to have

a talk," I tell Rue, and she nods, her eyes at half-mast as she gazes at me with need etched into her beautiful face.

She starts to wiggle and it takes me a second to realize that she's trying to get out of her yoga pants. We watch as she peels them down her legs, leaving just her thin cotton panties behind. I grit my teeth, holding back my bear when we see how soaked they are. The white fabric is basically see through and molded to the soft folds of her cunt.

"Fuck," I hiss out, and Liam licks his lips.

"I need a taste," he says, his voice coming out hoarse.

I nod, but he's already moving into place. He slips down her body, spreading her thighs wide so that he can settle between them.

His hands reach up, and I watch as he tears her panties, ripping them to shreds and tossing them over the side of the bed.

"So damn pretty," he murmurs, and Rue shifts, her thighs restless around his head.

"Liam... please," she begs, and he grins.

"You never have to beg me to lick this pretty pussy, sweetheart."

With that, he leans forward, burying his face in her sticky folds. He moans as her flavor hits his tongue, and my bear licks his lips. He can't wait until we get a turn to taste her.

I reach for her shirt and she lifts up, helping me pull it over her head. I reach for the clasp of her bra, tugging the straps down her arms. Her big tits bounce as she lays back on the mattress, staring up at me with those big blue eyes of hers.

"You're perfect," I whisper to her, and she nods, her mouth dropping open in a moan as Liam sucks her clit into his mouth.

"Let us make you feel good," I murmur to her as I cup her breasts.

I'm not sure that she heard me. She's too lost in her pleasure to pay attention to what I'm saying, and that's okay. I don't want to talk anymore anyway. I have better things to do with my mouth.

I lick one of her stiff nipples, sucking the peak into my mouth and rolling it against my tongue. Rue's head thrashes on the pillows, her hands fisting the sheets as her orgasm starts to hit her. I watch her as I switch to her other breast and give it the same treatment.

"Oh! Please!" Rue begs, and it only spurs us to double our efforts.

My bear and I can smell how close she is and when Liam leans back, taking two of his fingers to spank her clit, she goes flying over the edge.

"Yes!" She screams, and I grin, watching as she comes for us for the first time.

My cock is rock hard, demanding attention, but I can't let Liam have all the fun. I look at Liam, and he nods, letting me know to switch positions.

Rue blinks up at us as I settle between her thighs.

"My turn," I tell her darkly, and she swallows hard.

Liam cups her breasts and holds them up for his mouth as I lower my mouth to her delicious pussy.

With one lick, I'm addicted.

I suck her clit into my mouth, flicking my tongue over the small bundle of nerves there. Rue is moaning, her hands tearing at the sheets as she starts to rush toward another orgasm.

"Bo, Bo, Bo!" She chants, and I know that she's close.

I bury my face in her folds, licking and nipping along

her folds. My bear and I are in heaven now, and we want to wear her scent every day now.

"Give it to us," Liam orders her, and she splinters apart.

Her screams can probably be heard by all the Aspen Ridge Pack. My bear grins at that, wanting everyone to know that our mate is taken.

I give her pussy one last kiss before I crawl up her body and lay on her other side. She turns to me, trying to throw her leg over my waist, and I can't deny her anything.

"More," she begs, her snug hole brushing against my cock.

"We need to talk first," I tell her, my fingers gripping her hips to hold her in place.

If I wasn't in love with this girl before, I definitely am now. Her juices are still coating my face, her taste in my mouth. I just watched her come, and she still wants more. No, *needs* more. She's so horny for it. It's probably a good thing that there's two of us.

"Fuck me. Please," she begs, opening her eyes to look at me.

"No. We won't take you until you're wearing our marks. Until you agree to be ours forever," I tell her again, but it's so much harder to reject her this time.

"I need it, though. I need to feel you inside me," she pleads, her eyes widening as the stare into mine.

I don't know what to say, and my eyes lock with Liam's over her shoulder. I smirk at him, and he gives me a warning look. He looks intrigued, but a little wary, and I know that he's either going to love what I'm about to suggest or absolutely hate it.

"Alright, but we're going to talk while we do it," I tell Rue, and she nods eagerly.

I move, leaning up against the headboard of the bed,

and reach out, gripping her hips and pulling her on top of me. As soon as she's straddling me, I feel Rue start to rock on top of me, and my cock pulses as her juices start to cover me from root to tip. She moans, her face tipping up to the ceiling as her eyes flutter closed.

I glance behind her shoulder, grinning, when I see that Liam is kneeling between my legs behind her. His hands wrap around her, his hands finding her breasts and his fingers starting to toy with her tits, and I can't help but moan at the sight. Rue's eyes meet mine, her fingernails digging into my shoulders as her hips grind her pussy down against my dick.

"Come here, Rue," I say, gripping my cock as I help Rue kneel above me.

My cock points straight at her opening, desperate to get inside her snug channel. I shoot Rue a warning look when she tries to lower down on top of me, and she pouts but freezes.

"Alright, Rue. You're going to take the tip of me, okay? *Just* the tip," I stress, and Rue shakes her head frantically, her hips already starting to rock, greedy for my cock.

"Liam is going to keep you steady so that you don't take more."

My hands reach out, gripping her tight as she sinks down onto me. I groan, my mouth falling open as I watch the tip of my cock disappear between her glistening folds. Rue moans above me, and my mouth starts to water, wanting to lean forward and bite her right now.

Right, we need to talk during this.

How the hell am I going to remember to do that?

Liam smirks at me as he reaches around her, slipping his hand between her legs and finding that sensitive button.

"Oh!" Rue shouts as he starts to circle her clit.

Liam's other hand reaches up, cupping one of her breasts before his fingers toy with her nipple. I can feel Rue tightening around me already, her little pussy clamping down on the tip of my cock, and I lean forward, taking her other nipple into my mouth.

Liam and I work together to get our mate off, and we're rewarded a minute later when she tenses between us, crying out as her pussy pulses around me. Her juices run down my cock and coat me, and my bear screams at me to mark her now.

Mating heat. Fated mates. Have this conversation so we can claim her already, my bear snarls at me, and I pull away from her breast.

"Liam's turn," I rasp out, and Rue's eyes widen.

I pull her off my cock, helping her tilt forward so that Liam can line his cock up with her dripping opening. Liam pulls her into his lap, and she moans as she sinks down onto the tip of his erection. I shake my head, trying to push my bear down as I lean forward and suck her nipple into my mouth, using my other hand to rub her sweet pussy. It doesn't take long for Rue to start to tense once again, and I look down to see Liam's cock glistening with her cream.

You need to keep your head. Have this talk already!

"Tonight is that mating moon," I tell Rue, and she nods, her eyes trying to focus on me as Liam bounces her slightly on his dick. "That means that shifters feel this need to mate. We weren't sure if you were going to feel it too or not."

"I want you," she says, and I nod.

"You're going to get us," I tell her. "But we need to tell you about fated mates more first."

"Bo's turn," Liam says, a sheen of sweat on his forehead from holding himself and his bear back.

I move Rue back over my cock, and she sinks down

instantly. I grit my teeth, holding her in place so she can't take more of my pulsing length.

"Fated mates means forever. If we bite you, it means that you're ours," Liam explains.

"And we're yours," I add.

"Do you want that? Do you want to be ours forever?" Liam asks, and I freeze, holding my breath as we wait for our mate to answer.

"What happens if I say no?" She asks, seeming to come back to Earth for a second.

"Then we hit pause on this and try to show you that we're meant to be and that no one will love you more or treat you better than we will," I tell her.

She studies me for a moment before she turns to look back at Liam. I don't know what she sees on our faces or what seals it for us, but she nods.

"I don't want that," she whispers, and my heart kicks against my ribs.

My bear roars inside of me, happier than he's ever been.

"Thank you, baby," I tell her, and she gives me a small smile.

"We have to bite you now," Liam says, and she nods.

"Will it hurt?" She asks, worried about the pain.

"No. You actually might come," I tell her, and her eyes widen.

She nods, and I glance at Liam. He gives me a nod too.

We lean forward at the same time, and I lick my lips, letting my teeth elongate. Liam and I both take a deep breath before we lean forward and sink our teeth into the base of her neck.

Rue gasps, her body shivering as we mark her and make her ours.

"Bo, Liam," she says, her voice low and seductive.

We pull back, bothlicking the bite marks and sealing the wounds.

"You're ours now, mate," Liam says, and she nods.

"Now what?" She asks, her whole body flushed a beautiful shade of pink.

"Now we really fuck you," I tell her, and she giggles as I pull her between us.

Liam and I grin as we position our whole world between us.

ELEVEN

Rue

"LOOK AT WHAT YOU DID. Look at the mess you made," Bo says, and I glance down at their erections.

They're both red and angry looking and absolutely covered in my juices. The sight should make a virgin like me blush, but instead, all it does is turn me on.

"Do you want me to apologize, or do you want to make more of a mess?" I ask him and his eyes flare with arousal.

"You're fucking perfect for us," Liam purrs from behind me, and I shift against them, trying to get their cocks where I need them most.

I'm sandwiched between their hard bodies, and I love it. I've never felt so safe and loved in my whole life. My body feels like it's burning up, though, and I don't know if it's because of how hot they both are or because of how turned on I am right now.

My body is tingling, a dull ache starting between my legs. I press against them, and the same tingly feeling from early today roars to life inside me. My pussy clenches, begging to be filled.

"I need you," I beg them, and they nod.

Bo captures my lips with his, and I wrap my arms around his neck as Liam starts to trail kisses down my spine. I shiver as his hot breath fans against my skin, and Bo grins against my lips.

"We're going to take such good care of you, baby," he promises, and I nod.

They keep me balanced on my side as Bo starts to kiss down my front, and I grip the pillow under my head, hanging on as their mouths do wicked things to me.

Their hands glide up my legs as their mouths move down, and my brain almost short-circuits. I'm not sure what to focus on as their lips, tongue, and teeth continue to work me over.

It feels like I'm being branded, and I start to pant as they near the juncture of my thighs. They spread my legs wide, resting my legs on their shoulders and making room to accommodate both of them.

Liam uses his fingers to spread my lower lips, and they both groan when they see how wet I am for them. I look down, and I can't help but moan when I see them lick their lips.

Then they're moving as one.

Bo leans forward, licking up my center and swirling his tongue around my sensitive clit. I cry out, almost arching off the bed as they start to eat me out.

"We need to make sure that you're wet enough for us," Bo says with a grin, and I want to curse him out.

"I am," I promise him, but he just dips his head, his tongue finding me once more.

Bo's mouth opens over my pussy, and he starts to eat at

me like a man starved. His tongue lashes against my clit before it dips down to my opening. As soon as Bo's mouth moves away, Liam's fingers are there to rub my wet flesh and offer pleasure. They work as a team to drive me closer and closer to the edge, and I scream their names as my orgasm finally hits me.

I can feel my pussy pulsing against Bo's tongue, my eyes falling shut as I come harder than I have in my entire life. I feel the bed shift, and I come back down to Earth, blinking my eyes open to see them both crawling up the bed toward me.

They lay on their sides on either side of me, and I writhe when I feel their hands start to run along my body. My skin is so overstimulated that I feel like I could come again just from them breathing on me.

They stroke up my stomach, making me giggle and twitch between them. When their hands reach my breasts, my smile drops off, and all I can do is moan. I gasp as they rub me, and I can feel another orgasm starting to build deep in my core. I reach up, fisting my hands in their hair, and they both lean down. My lips meet Bo's and I can taste my juices on his lips. I moan at the flavor only to have Liam grip my chin and turn my face to meet his.

Liam pulls away, and they both stare down at me, brushing some of my hair away from my neck and shoulders. Anticipation thunders through my bloodstream like a herd of horses, and I arch my chest up, offering them my body.

"Fuck me," I order, a flush blooming on my cheeks and working down to the tops of my tits.

Liam settles between my legs, gripping my thighs and holding me open as he lines his thick cock up with my opening. I watch him, tangling my hand in Bo's hair as he leans down to nuzzle his bite mark. A baby orgasm pulses through me, and I look up at Liam, raising my hips to him in invitation.

"You're ours now," Liam tells me.

"Finally," Bo adds.

Liam thrusts forward, tearing through my innocence, and I cry out, but Bo is there to help ease the pain. His fingers pluck and toy with my nipples as he licks, rolling the stiff peaks between his fingers. He trails kisses up and down my neck, and every time he gets close to his mark, a tiny orgasm rushes through me.

My pussy clenches around Liam's length, and I moan as he starts to move inside me. He rocks against me, moving slowly at first until I get used to the feeling of being stuffed so fully.

"More. It feels so good," I moan after a couple of minutes, and I feel both of their grips tighten on me.

Bo starts to pinch my nipples, using more pressure as Liam begins to pound into me. He ruts between my legs like an animal, and I arch against him, loving every minute of it. Our bodies fit together so perfectly. My legs are tangled around his waist, and I realize that the higher my legs climb on Liam's waist, the deeper he thrusts inside of me.

"You going to come for him?" Bo asks me as Liam thrusts harder into me, and I can only nod.

I moan, throwing my head back as his words send a fresh rush of desire flooding through me. I work my legs up onto Liam's shoulders, and he grabs my ankles, pushing my feet towards my head and holding me open to him. Bo's hand slips down between my legs, and he finds my clit, rubbing in tight circles as I start to cry out their names.

"That's it, baby. Such a good little girl," Bo says, and that's all it takes.

My pussy clamps down around Liam's length as I come. I scream his name, moaning it over and over again as my greedy pussy pulls Liam's orgasm from him. He shouts my name as he comes inside me, and I whine and spasm around him as he fills me up.

It feels like our orgasms go on for hours, but it was probably only seconds. Still, I hate when Liam starts to pull away. He leans down and brushes his mouth against mine as he pulls out of me slowly. He kisses me deeply as he rolls onto his side, and then Bo is taking his spot between my legs.

"Are you ready for me?" Bo asks, and I nod my head frantically.

I'm a little sore, but I want both of them. A fresh wave of need floods my body when I see Bo between my thighs, and I notice his eyes darken even more.

"The pull is only going to get stronger," Liam says quietly, and Bo curses under his breath.

"What does that mean?" I ask.

"You're going to get horny. Really, really horny," Bo says as he starts to push his thick cock inside me.

Bo starts to move inside me as Liam nips and licks his way across my tits. I moan as Bo sinks into me, his balls slapping my ass as he pounds into me over and over again. Liam's fingers brush over the marks they left on me, and I arch as a little orgasm rolls through me. My pussy tightens further around Bo, and that only spurs him to fuck me harder.

"More, more, more," I plead with him.

"I promise that we are going to fuck you in every imaginable position tonight, mate," Liam whispers in my ear as he continues to tease my tits.

I whimper at his words, my desire bumping up a couple

of notches as Bo glides in and out of me. I'm so wet that I can hear it as Bo continues to grind against me.

"Fuck," Liam breathes as he watches Bo fuck me.

"You're so fucking hot," Bo moans, and I arch into him, wanting Liam's mouth back on me.

He seems to get the memo because his lips wrap around one stiff peak, and he sucks it into his mouth, flicking his tongue back and forth over the bud. I feel myself start to splinter apart, and I suck in a deep breath, letting it out in a scream as I come all over Bo's cock. My orgasm triggers his own, and I feel Bo come inside me, his release hot and sticky as it splashes off my walls.

Bo rolls off of me, cradling me against his chest, and I sigh deeply, my body exhausted.

"We need to feed you," Liam says, and Bo nods.

"What are you hungry for?" He asks.

"Macaroni and cheese," I say instantly, and they grin.

"We can do that. Why don't you take a bath and soak for a bit?" Bo suggests.

"I'll get the water started," Liam says, already springing out of bed.

I watch him go, and I want to argue, to tell him that I can run myself a bath just fine, but he's already turning the water on.

"That was incredible," Bo whispers to me, his teeth nipping the shell of my ear.

"Will it always be like that?" I ask him, and he nods.

"We'll always make it good for you, baby. Even when we take you here," he says, his fingers rimming my back door.

My mouth drops open, and I can feel my face turning as red as my hair, but I'm not scared for them to do that. In fact, I'm kind of looking forward to trying.

"We'll go get you that macaroni and cheese," he says, dropping one last kiss on my lips before he climbs out of bed.

I watch them both go before I crawl out of bed and head into the bathroom. The bath is almost overflowing with bubbles, and I sigh as I let my tired body sink into the hot water.

I wonder if we can make love again after we eat...

My eyes fly open at that thought, and it hits me then just how much they have come to mean to me in such a short amount of time.

I like the way they look out for me, how they're always checking me out and making sure I have everything that I need. I love the way they make me feel like I'm protected and safe and like I'm the most precious thing in the world to them. They make me feel cherished and loved.

I love them.

I don't want to leave them. I want to belong to them, to be their mate.

But now that the post-orgasmic bliss is starting to fade, I can't help but wonder if being their mate means trading in one cage for another.

I wanted to be on my own. I wanted to escape the overbearing man in my life. Did I really do that? Or did I just trade my father for two more jailers?

TWELVE

Liam

WE'VE CLAIMED and bitten our mate. We've made love to her. This should be the happiest moment in our lives. Things should be smooth sailing.

But they're not.

There's something going on with our mate. I can't quite pinpoint when, but Rue has started to pull back from us. Bo and I have both noticed it; I can tell. He's on edge, just like me.

"What did we do?" He whispers to me as he joins me in the kitchen.

"I don't know. When did you start to notice that she was pulling back from us?" I ask him, and he shakes his head.

"I didn't. Not until this morning when we woke up, and she wasn't in bed with us anymore."

"Same. She seemed happy last night," I murmur, trying to remember if anything had seemed amiss after we made love to her last night.

"Maybe it was just too much for her too fast?" Bo suggests, and I shake my head.

"I don't know. She seemed into it last night. Both times. I guess that you could be right, though."

We both mull over what could have happened as we start to pull out a few things for lunch. Neither of us is that hungry, but I don't know what else to do. Besides, we needed a reason to break off and talk about what could be going on.

I grab the stuff to make sandwiches, and we work in silence for a few minutes. Once we have the sandwiches ready, I turn to Bo.

"We should just come out and ask her. We're going to drive both of us crazy if we keep worrying about it. Plus, maybe it's something that she's stressed about, and we can put her at ease too," I tell him.

"Okay. I'll follow your lead," he says, and I take a deep breath before we grab the plates and head back to the living room.

The peace that I had found at knowing that we're about to clear all of this up is short-lived, though.

When we get back to the living room, it's empty. I frown, glancing over at Bo, but he looks just as clueless.

"Did she go upstairs?" He asks.

I turn, about to go check, when I notice the snow already melting on the floor by the front door.

"Shit!" I shout, dropping the plates onto the coffee table and rushing over to the front door.

Bo has caught on, too, and we both race outside, our hearts racing and our bears on high alert inside of us as we search for her.

"Why would she run off?" I ask.

"Again," he adds.

She's headed for the forest this time, and we take off after her. It doesn't take us long to catch up with her, and I reach out, grabbing her arm and tugging her to a stop.

"Rue," Bo starts, and I search her face.

"What's wrong?"

She has tears already streaming down her face, and the sight breaks my heart.

"Baby, what happened?" Bo asks, pulling her into his arms.

"I can't... I can't do this," she sobs, the dam breaking and a fresh wave of tears falling from her eyes.

"It's freezing out here. We need to get you back inside," I say, and she shakes her head.

"No, I need to go."

"No," I say stubbornly.

"Why?" Bo asks, looking heartbroken.

"This is all just too much. It's reminding me of my father, and I promised that I would never go back to that," she says, trying to wipe her eyes.

"What does that mean?" I ask.

"He... my father wasn't a good man. Maybe he was at one point, but I never saw that side of him. He was cruel. He barely looked or talked to me, and when he did, it was never to be nice."

Bo and I share a look. Neither of us can figure out how we would remind her of her father.

"He used to lock me in my closet or the basement. I wasn't allowed to work or go out besides school. I thought I would be trapped there with him forever, but I saved, and I got out."

"Good," I say, and she looks down at her feet.

"I promised myself that I would start over somewhere

new, that I would be independent and that I wouldn't let another man make all of my decisions for me."

Bo and I share another look, the puzzle pieces starting to click for both of us.

"I want to stand on my own two feet. I want to make my own decisions," she says, and I swallow hard.

"We can do that," I say, and she gives me a skeptical look.

"We can," Bo promises. "We promise. We'll do anything for you."

"We just want what's best for you, Rue. We just want to make you happy," I tell her, and she nods.

"I know you do. It's just... I need to be alone right now. I need time to think."

She's practically begging us to understand, and my bear growls inside me. He doesn't want to let Rue out of our sight, but what choice do we have? We want her to be happy. We've already practically held her captive once, and we promised her then that we would let her go if she just gave us a few days.

"Okay, take all of the time that you need. Just do it here. Do it at our place, where we know that you'll be safe."

"I can't," she starts, but I cut her off.

"It's fine. We'll go stay with Ryder."

"I can't kick you out of your home," she argues.

"Rue, it's not a home without you there."

Bo nods, looking as devastated as I feel. At least as long as she's at our place, we know that she's safe and comfortable. I think my bear and I would go crazy if we didn't know where she was and if she was okay.

"Take all the time that you need," I tell Rue, pulling her into my arms and tipping her face up to mine.

My lips claim hers, and I try to pour all my feelings for

her into this one last kiss. I know that she can feel this connection between us too. I just hope that she remembers it when she's alone.

I break off the kiss and step back, letting Bo take my place. He kisses her, too, his hands holding her tight, and I know that it's going to kill him to have to let her go.

We walk Rue back to the house, and I head upstairs to pack me and Bo a bag of clothes. I grab enough for three days. I'm hoping that Rue doesn't need more than that.

My bear paces back and forth inside me. He doesn't understand why we're leaving. He wants to stay and fight for her. He doesn't understand that giving her space is our best bet at being able to keep her.

I head back downstairs and see Bo looking forlorn by the front door. He takes the bag from me, turning to open the door, and I turn back to see Rue watching us with big, sad eyes.

"We'll do anything for you, sweetheart. We're not your father, and we would never treat you like that. Take all the time that you need."

She nods, and I see a fresh wave of tears fill her eyes. It kills me not to go to her then and comfort her, but I force myself to turn and follow Bo out the door.

We share one heartbroken look before we turn and head toward Ryder's place.

THIRTEEN

Bo

I THOUGHT NOT BEING able to find my mate was hell. I was wrong. Finding Rue and then losing her is so much worse.

Liam and I have been moping around Ryder's house for the last two days. Sienna has been doing her best to cheer us up, but none of it is working. We both just keep wondering what Rue could be doing and if she's missing us.

"We could go for another run," Liam half-heartedly suggests.

We've been going for runs at least twice a day. It helps to let our bears out to burn off some energy, and it helps us to pass the time. We also may have been running by our place. Just to see if we could spot her. So far, we've only seen her once, and she was pacing back and forth in front of the window.

Ryder stomps past, giving us a dirty look, but we ignore him. He hasn't been thrilled that we're here with them, and

I get it. He just mated with Sienna last month, and I'm sure he wants to keep her all to himself.

He's a good friend, though, so he's been letting us crash in his guest room. Now that it's been a few days, I can tell that he wants us to make up with Rue almost as much as we do.

We promised to give our mate space, but I don't think that Bo and I can take much more than this. I just wish that we could talk to her. We need to figure out how to fix this so we can go back to doing everything to make Rue happy and safe.

We'd have to talk to our mate to figure that out, though, and she hasn't shown any sign of being ready to see us yet.

Please, God, let her be ready soon.

Liam lets out another sigh, and I stare at the ceiling. My bear is an angry beast inside of me. He's been pacing, growling, and swiping at me ever since we walked away from Rue the other day.

"Why don't you two just go check on your mate," Ryder suggests, and I see Sienna give him a warning look.

"We promised to give her space," Liam says.

Ryder sighs, and Sienna elbows him.

"Wait... does Rue know where you are?" Sienna asks, and I nod.

"Yeah, we told her we were staying here with Ryder," I tell her.

"Right, but does she know where Ryder lives?" She asks, and I blink.

"I..." Liam starts, frowning as he looks over at me.

"No," I state. "She doesn't. She just knows that he's close by."

"Okay, so how is she supposed to contact you if she

wants to talk?" She asks us. "Does she have your phone numbers? Or our phone number?"

"No... we don't even have hers," Liam says as he sits up straighter on the couch.

His black hair is flattened on one side, the side he's been lying on for the last few hours. Dark circles are under his blue eyes, and he looks just as exhausted as I do.

The plows came by this morning and cleaned off the paths and people's porches. Rue could try to come find us... or she could try to leave.

"We need to go check on her," I blurt out, and Liam nods.

We both leap to our feet and say a distracted goodbye to Ryder and Sienna before we race out the door. I can feel the excitement coming off of Liam in waves, and I smile for the first time in what feels like years as we race back home.

For the first time in days, my bear is calm inside me. He's standing motionless as I sprint back to the house. It's almost like he's holding his breath, waiting to take another one until we're face to face with our Rue again.

My bear is just as anxious and excited to see Rue as we are.

I can only hope our mate is as happy to see us as we are to see her.

FOURTEEN

Rue

I KNEW I had made a mistake as soon as the door closed behind Liam and Bo. I don't know why I pushed them away. I don't want to live without my men.

I felt like such an idiot after what I had said to them. I mean, comparing my mates to my father? They're nothing alike. Comparing them to him wasn't fair to them. My men are so sweet and good to me. They're kind and patient. They would never say or do anything to hurt or upset me. Seeing me cry tears them up inside.

They care about me. They *love* me. And I love them. I was just too scared to admit that. Now I may have messed everything up.

How am I going to make this up to them?

I've been waiting for them to come back. When they didn't return the second day, I realized that they might not for a while. I have no idea where they are or how to get in contact with them. I was hoping that they would stop back to check on me and I could tell them that I made a mistake and fix this, but that hasn't happened.

I'm going to have to go into town. Maybe someone can point me in the right direction, or maybe someone has their phone numbers and I can call them to tell them to come home.

With that plan in place, I tug my jacket and shoes on. Before I can, though, there's a knock on the door.

I know instantly that it's Bo and Liam, and my heart leaps in my chest. I run to answer the door, ripping it open, and there they are.

I do two things simultaneously then.

The first is that I burst into tears.

The second is that I launch myself at them, wrapping my arms around their necks.

"Rue! What's wrong?" Liam asks, sounding panicked.

I can feel Bo looking around, trying to find what upset me.

"Are they inside?" Liam asks, and I pull back.

"What?"

"Why are you crying? Are they inside? Are you okay?"

"I'm fine," I promise them, and they look at me like I'm crazy.

"Why are you crying, baby?" Bo asks, wiping the tears from my cheeks.

Liam picks me up, carrying me inside, and I start to cry harder. Man, I missed them. I missed them picking me up and carrying me around like I weigh nothing.

They always made me feel so safe and so cherished. I'm a curvy girl, but they act like I am light as a feather. I missed them so much.

"Calm down, sweetheart," Liam begs, and I nod, wrapping my arms around his neck and clinging to him as he sits down on the couch.

Bo sits next to us, his hands rubbing my back in soothing circles. They're both trying to calm me down, and I know they hate seeing me cry, so I try to get myself under control.

"We'll go. We'll give you more time. We just wanted to check on you," Bo says, and I shake my head.

"No!" I shout firmly. "Please don't go."

"Has everything been okay here?" Liam asks, his green eyes darting around.

"I'm so sorry," I tell them, and they frown, sharing a confused look.

"For what?" Bo asks.

"For saying all of that stuff the other day. For pushing you both away. I just got scared, and I tried to ruin what we have. Please don't go away again."

"Rue," Bo starts.

"I love you. I love both of you," I tell them, and they freeze.

"Say it again," Liam orders, and I swallow hard.

"I love you, Liam. I love you, Bo. So much."

Tears sting the back of my eyes, and I brush them away. I don't think I've cried this much before in my life.

"I want to be with you," I tell them, and they both beam at me.

"Thank god," Bo says, burying his face in my neck to nuzzle my bite mark. "We love you too."

"So much, sweetheart," Liam adds

"We were going crazy without you," Bo says.

"It was awful. I never want to be away from you again," Liam adds, his lips finding mine.

He kisses me, and I sink into him, letting him take the lead. He licks against the seam of my lips, and I open for him, greedy to taste him again. I'm getting lost in Liam when Bo's fingers grip my chin, and he turns me in his direction.

I smile as I kiss Bo back, loving how desperate they both seem for me.

"Maybe we should take this upstairs," I suggest when Liam turns my head back to him.

"You're a genius, mate," Bo says, and I giggle as Liam lifts me in his arms and the three of us head up to our bedroom.

Being in this house without them felt so wrong, and I'm just grateful to have them back where they belong.

With me.

FIFTEEN

Bo

ONE YEAR LATER...

"HOW'S YOUR MOM?" Rue asks as soon as I walk in the door.

"She's doing great," I tell Liam and my mate.

They both relax, and I grin as I head over to rub Rue's swollen stomach. She's about eight months along, and the doctor warned against traveling so soon to her due date, so I went to Anchorage by myself this month while Liam stayed home with our mate.

My mom is doing a lot better, and she got the all-clear to travel from her doctors. She's so excited that she'll be able to come here once the baby is born, and I can't wait to have our family all together under one roof.

Liam's mom is equally excited about being a grandma. Between the two of them, we've got enough diapers and baby clothes to last us until the kid is ten at least. I love that they want to spend time with and spoil our kid, though, and I know they're going to be great grandparents.

"How was your day here?" I ask Rue as I bend down to kiss her stomach.

"Boring. Liam won't let me do anything," she complains, and I share a smile with my best friend.

"Like what?" I ask her.

"Like cook, do the dishes or laundry, shovel the front porch," Liam rattles off.

"It was just the steps!" Rue tries to argue, but he shakes his head.

We both have a hard time saying no to our mate, but when it comes to her safety, we manage to.

"Let me rub your feet," I tell her as I lead her over to the couch.

"Liam already did that. Besides, nothing is going to help with the swelling. Not until I get this baby out of me," she says, cupping her round belly.

"Soon, baby," I tell her, tugging her down onto the sofa.

I grab her feet while Liam starts to massage her shoulders, and Rue moans.

"Alright, it does feel good," she says.

I smile at that. Rue is still so independent, and I know this pregnancy has been hard on her. She's been doing great, though, and I know that she's aware that Liam and I would do anything for her. Sometimes that means foot rubs or running to the store at odd hours, and sometimes that means taking turns licking her sweet pussy until she forgets about how uncomfortable she is. Either way, Liam and I are more than happy to take care of any of her needs.

We tied the knot a few months ago in a small ceremony in Anchorage. That way, our parents were able to come. We told them then that we were also expecting and the whole weekend turned into one big celebration.

After that, we whisked Rue off to Hawaii. We got to lay around in the sun or splash in the ocean. I just love that we got to see Rue in so many bikinis. We ruined more than a few of them by ripping them off her whenever we were alone, but she didn't seem to mind much.

Rue's settled in here, especially once her best friend moved here after she was mated with Roman. She's gotten closer to Sienna, too, and now the girls get together to hang out almost every single day.

Iggy was just supposed to come out for a visit but ended up falling in love and staying. I know that Rue is happy about that. She was missing her best friend.

We never heard from her father. I know that Rue was worried about that in the beginning, but he never tried to find her or reach out. It's his loss. She's the best thing to ever happen to him or anyone, and he was just too stupid to realize that.

There are a few snowflakes coming down, and I make a mental note to grab some more firewood from outside just in case it starts to storm tonight.

A knock sounds at the door, and I let Liam answer it.

"Hey," he greets Sienna and Iggy.

Both girls come rushing in, their arms full of pickles and salt and vinegar Pringles. It's what all three of them seem to be craving their whole pregnancies. We have a ton more stocked in the pantry.

"Where's Ryder and Roman?" Liam asks when he realizes that it's just the girls here.

"I'm sure that they're not far behind," Iggy says as she rushes over to one of the chairs and collapses into it.

Her hands go to her pregnant belly, and I look at Liam

to see him already texting their mates to let them know they're here.

"Are you ladies thirsty?" I ask, and they nod.

"Do you have any hot chocolate?" Iggy asks.

"Oh, yeah! You guys have the best hot chocolate here," Sienna says with a moan.

"I know! Roman tried to buy it, but for some reason, it just tastes better here," Iggy says.

"Real whip cream," Rue tells her, and Iggy sighs.

"That's probably it. Roman has been obsessed with that almond milk kind, but it's just not as good."

"It's better for you," Roman tells her as he comes inside, followed closely by Ryder.

"I told you to stay put and that I would walk you over," Ryder grumbles, and Sienna just grins at him.

Liam comes out of the kitchen carrying three hot chocolates and some bottles of water. Rue smiles up at him, her hand almost connecting with the mug when she gasps, bending over as her hands go to cradle her stomach.

Liam and I are on her at once.

"Rue?" I ask.

"What's wrong?" Liam asks.

She takes a deep breath, her eyes squeezed shut, and we both turn to Roman. He's a doctor at the hospital here in Aspen Ridge.

"How long have you been having contractions?" He asks as he moves to check her out.

"An hour or so," she says.

"What?" Liam half shouts. "Why didn't you say anything?"

"They were just little ones, and besides, I wanted to wait for Bo to get back."

"Well, I'm here now. We need to get you to the hospital."

Roman nods, and I run upstairs to grab the hospital bag and car seat out of the nursery. We packed it just last week, and now I'm glad we didn't put it off any longer.

"Ready?" Liam asks as I come back downstairs, and I nod.

Iggy and Sienna are both hugging Rue goodbye and promising to come by to check on her soon. We wave at our friends as we usher Rue out the door and over to the SUV.

We never saw the point in owning a car. We could just walk or run anywhere we needed to go, but with Rue and the baby, we bought one.

I toss the bags into the backseat as Liam gets her comfortable in the passenger seat. We both climb in, and then we're off. I grip Rue's hand, trying to remember the breathing techniques as Liam races toward the hospital.

"It's okay, baby. We've got you," I tell her, and she smiles.

"I know."

"Love you, Rue," Liam says, and she grins.

"I know. I love you two too. Now, let's go have this baby!"

I laugh, sharing a smile with Liam in the rear-view mirror as we get ready to welcome the newest member of our family into the world.

9 798215 883037